# Permian Field Guide
## 299-250 million years ago

Cotylorhynchus

Proterosuchus

Edaphosaurus

Secondontosaurus

Disclaimer: THERE ARE NO DINOSAURS IN THIS BOOK.
Everything found in this book is from the Permian time period. Use the field guide
in this book to discover the amazing animals that lived before the dinosaurs.
— DDjr.

## immedium
inspiring a world of imagination

Immedium, Inc.
P.O. Box 31846
San Francisco, CA 94131
www.immedium.com

Text and Illustrations
Copyright © 2014 David G. Derrick, Jr.

First hardcover edition published 2014.

Edited by Tracy Swedlow
Book design by Joy Liu
Hand lettering by Robert C. Trujillo

Printed in Malaysia
10 9 8 7 6 5 4 3 2 1

Library of Congress Cataloging-in-Publication Data

Derrick, David G., 1978- author, illustrator.
Play with your food / by David G. Derrick, Jr. -- First edition.
pages cm
Summary: "In the prehistoric Permian Period, a small reptile tries to convince a larger and
hungry dimetrodon to not eat it, but to play with its food instead"-- Provided by publisher.
ISBN 978-1-59702-102-9 (hardback) -- ISBN 1-59702-102-4 (hardcover)
[1. Dimetrodon--Fiction. 2. Dinosaurs--Fiction. 3. Prehistoric animals--Fiction.
4. Play--Fiction. 5. Games--Fiction.] I. Title. PZ7.D4465Pl 2014 [E]--dc23 2014008729

ISBN: 978-1-59702-102-9

# Play with your Food

## By David G. Derrick, Jr.

immedium

Immedium, Inc.
San Francisco, CA

**BLZz**

Meal time in the Permian
was an eat-or-be-eaten world.

Whew!
That was close.

Have you ever tried
playing with your food instead?

Why that's the silliest thing I've ever heard. **Play with your food?** No one plays with their food — they eat it.

Oh believe you me, it's the funnest thing you can do with your food.

Well, we could play...

Peek a... Boo!

We could
draw,

play music,

play
I SPY,

or Pick-up
Sticks!